Sarah Is Scared!

And Other Really Good Reasons to HAVE FAITH

Written and illustrated by
Sandy Silverthorne

Equipping Kids For Life!

To my southern California family:
Gary, Patti, Angi, Jessi, Jordan, Kate, Rex, and Erik.
We treasure our times with you.

FaithKids® is an imprint of Cook Communications Ministries,
Colorado Springs, Colorado 80918
Cook Communications, Paris, Ontario
Kingsway Communications, Eastbourne, England

SARAH IS SCARED!
© 2001 by Sandy Silverthorne for text and illustrations

Designed by iDesignEtc.
Edited by Kathy Davis

First hardcover printing, 2001
Printed in Singapore
05 04 03 02 01   5 4 3 2 1

It's not as if Sarah was scared of **everything** ...

...just dogs and lightning and scary movies and the dark and new people and bugs and school and ivy and paper clips and snow and what may be under her bed and 8 track tapes and cellos...well, you get the idea.

Sarah was born in Korea and was adopted when she was really little. Her new parents flew all the way over to Seoul to meet her and bring her home.

But for some reason she's always been scared of all kinds of things. Once in science, they talked about spontaneous combustion: the phenomenon where an object just bursts into flames for no reason.

HOW IT WORKS:

Random Object

1 minute later

That scared Sarah for about a month.

Sometimes it wasn't a good idea for Sarah to
play scary video games...

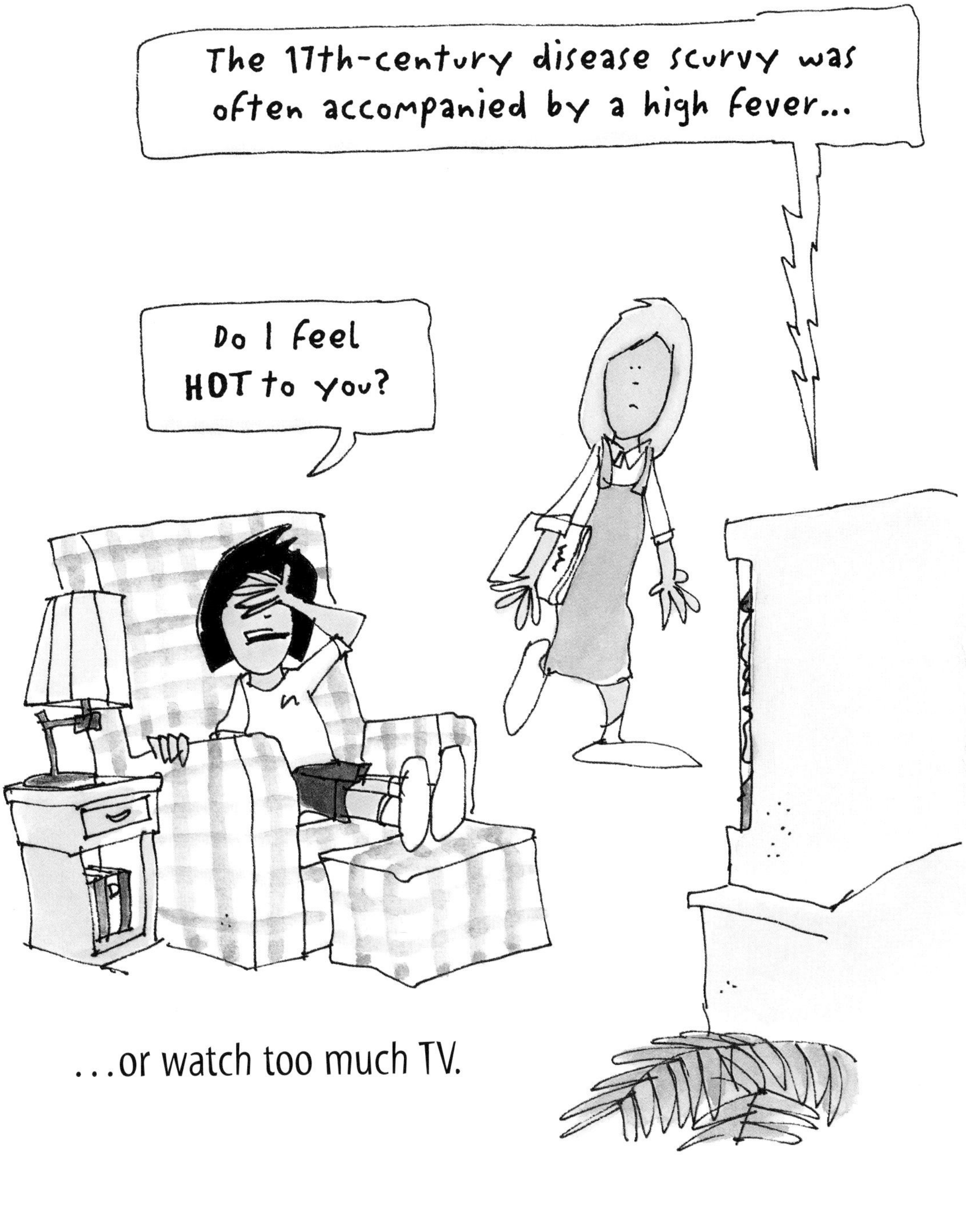

...or watch too much TV.

Sarah had gone to Sunday school all her life. She knew in her head that God was committed to taking care of her, but her feelings didn't always feel that way.

Almost all the kids in Sarah's neighborhood were in the same Sunday school class. They loved their teachers Mr. and Mrs. Fleece.

Today the class was talking about faith.

The kids were split up into three discussion groups with the question "What is faith?" Sarah looked around. Her group was Christy, Gregory, Tyler, Marpel and herself. Surely if any group on earth could come up with the definition of faith, it would be this one.

As usual, Marpel started the discussion. She spoke with authority. "Faith is believing something you know to be absolutely untrue!"

At first everyone sat staring in shocked silence. Then Gregory spoke up. "No it isn't, faith is believing God even when you don't know how it's gonna turn out." That was good. Sarah was getting interested.

Christy chimed in. "Like one time my dad said he was taking us somewhere special on Saturday. And even though I didn't know what or where, I saved the whole day 'cause I knew he was gonna do it."

"Where'd he take you?" the kids asked.

"To Captain Kidd's Fun Zone and Putt-Putt golf center."

"Oooooooh," the group added.

"So, if we're facing something scary," said Sarah, "we pray and trust that God's gonna meet us there."

"Just like Christy's dad," said Gregory.

FORE!

When the class came back together and shared their ideas, Mrs. Fleece said, "Those were all very good. Now we want to tell you about some spies in the Bible."

Spies? In the Bible?

That got everyone's attention. Especially when Mr. Fleece appeared in a trenchcoat, hat and sunglasses.

"A long time ago, God used Moses to lead the Israelites out of Egypt. They spent time in the desert and they journeyed until they were on the border of the Promised Land. That's when Moses decided to send twelve spies ahead to see what this new land was like. The spies spent forty days in the land and came back with their report. After all the people gathered around, ten of the spies gave their report. . . .

...It was terrifying!"

"I knew it," whispered Sarah to Christy.

Mr. Fleece continued. "The spies said, 'There were big, powerful, scary, giant people defending the land! Why, they were so big, we *felt like grasshoppers* in comparison!'"

"I know just how they feel. I hate that!" shouted Sarah. The whole class was quiet for a minute while everyone looked at Sarah.

"Ahem," said Mr. Fleece, continuing. "But there were two spies, Joshua and Caleb, who disagreed with the others. 'That's right, the people there are big and strong,' they said, 'But the land is rich and wonderful! Besides, God is with us—**and nobody can fight against the Lord and win!**'"

"But the people were scared. They didn't have faith. That is, they didn't believe God could help them so they gave up and ended up wandering around the desert for forty years!"

"I bet they didn't even have sufficient sunscreen," commented Sarah, who had just seen an infomercial on skin care.

Sarah really liked Mr. Fleece's story and started to realize that the way to have faith is to believe God and to do what He wants you to do, even if it seems scary.

She felt pretty good for awhile *until* the big announcement at her Tapawinga Girls' Troop meeting. It seemed the whole troop was going to go camping at Lake Catchatoomie! In the out-of-doors! In the forsaken wilderness!

Sarah's heart sank.

That's just the type of thing that made her *really* scared.

Sarah's mind flashed to a TV program she had just seen on all the man-eating animals and fish of the world. She was *positive* their campsite was mentioned several times.

Being at the mercy of the wilderness made Sarah feel as small as a grasshopper. When she told her parents, they said, "We know this is the kind of thing that scares you but it'll be good for you. Besides, God's going to help you."

The trip to the lake was about an hour and a half.

Almost everyone on the bus had
an enjoyable time.

After Sarah got there, she actually was having a pretty good time. There was a lake, really fun games and even horses! They also had a big suspension bridge that went across the ravine.

All the kids loved running and jumping on it.

Sarah thought it would be a good idea to take down that rickety old bridge and put up a more solid structure. Perhaps a big steel or concrete bridge would do the trick.

On Wednesday, Sarah went out in a canoe with her best friend, Christy. It was kind of fun, except that Sarah was sure she saw a school of man-eating fish following them.

That afternoon, Mrs. Dockmeister asked if Sarah would watch her youngest daughter, Brittany, for the afternoon.

Brittany and Sarah explored the whole camp together.

As they walked around the back of the kitchen, they suddenly stopped short. Look at that! It was a raccoon! He was looking around for scraps of food. He was so busy he didn't even notice the two girls standing there.

"Wow," whispered Sarah. "You stay here. I want to get my camera in the cabin. Don't move, I'll be right back." Brittany watched the raccoon for a minute then started to sit down.

The movement made the little animal look up and see Brittany. He didn't like to be watched while he ate, so he headed back into the woods. Not wanting to lose him, Brittany followed.

A few minutes later Sarah returned, but of course there was no raccoon and no Brittany! Sarah started searching frantically.

She followed the little path through the woods until she came to the suspension bridge.

BRIDGE

CABINS

LAKE

Of course. There was Brittany, right in the middle of the bridge, scared and crying. "It had to be the bridge," sighed Sarah.

"Well, God was able to help those Israelites, I guess He can help me get across this bridge!" she thought to herself. "It's okay!" called Sarah as she edged toward the bridge. "I'm here, I'll help you get off."

"All right, Lord, I'm going to help Brit.
But You've gotta help me...
Okay...

...I'm stepping out on the bridge now. Now I'm
walking a little farther...

...I'm getting closer to the middle. Hope you
don't mind if I don't look down. One more step."

(After this was all over, Sarah realized that God knew all
along what she was doing but it somehow made her
feel better to be talking to Him as she went.)

Finally! She got to Brittany! Sarah held onto her real tight as they made it back to the side. "There. See, Brittany? The bridge isn't that scary!" (Sarah was really talking to herself at that point.)

That night at the campfire everybody clapped when they heard how Sarah saved Brittany off the bridge.

She even got the first-ever "I can do all things through Christ who strengthens me" award, also known as the "Tapawinga Girls' No-Longer-A-Grasshopper Award."

Sarah felt really good that the Lord had showed her that her faith was growing—*and* she was able to do the hard things she needed to...

...even in the forsaken wilderness.

Sarah Is Scared!
And Other Really Good Reasons to Have Faith

Ages: 4-7

Life Issue: My child is learning to depend on God
in the everyday situations of life.

Spiritual Building Block: Faith

Learning Styles
Help your child learn about God's Word in the following ways:

Sight: With your child look again at the picture of Sarah's Sunday school class. Ask: "Who had the wrong idea about faith?" (Marpel did; she said faith is believing something that is untrue.) Have your child point to the kids with a good understanding of faith. (Gregory and Christy both knew that faith means trusting God even when you aren't sure of the outcome.) Encourage your child to tell you about a time he or she trusted God.

Sound: Talk with your child about the theme of this story: When we are afraid, we should pray and trust that God will be with us. Explain that Sarah was afraid of many things, in the same way that your child has his or her own fears. Ask your child to talk about the scary things he or she faces. Then pray together and ask God to reassure your child about His care and presence. Help your child memorize Philippians 4:13: "I can do all things through Christ who strengthens me" (NKJV).

Touch: Plan a "trust walk" with your child to demonstrate the concept of faith. After explaining what you will do, blindfold your child, hold hands, and lead him or her on a walk through your home or yard. Give careful directions—such as "step up here" or "we will be turning now"—so that your child will move safely. Afterward, ask your child to trust you as you feed him or her a favorite treat, sight unseen. Then talk about your child's feeling about trusting without seeing.